Each Puffin Easy-to-Read book has a color-coded reading level to make book selection easy for parents and children. Because all children are unique in their reading development, Puffin's three levels make it easy for teachers and parents to find the right book to suit each individual child's reading readiness.

Level 1: Short, simple sentences full of word repetition—plus clear visual clues to help children take the first important steps toward reading.

Level 2: More words and longer sentences for children just beginning to read on their own.

Level 3: Lively, fast-paced text—perfect for children who are reading on their own.

*"Readers aren't born, they're made.
Desire is planted—planted by
parents who work at it."*

—**Jim Trelease**, author of
The Read-Aloud Handbook

For Carol Nicklaus

PUFFIN BOOKS
Published by the Penguin Group
Penguin Books USA Inc., 375 Hudson Street, New York, New York 10014, U.S.A.
Penguin Books Ltd, 27 Wrights Lane, London W8 5TZ, England
Penguin Books Australia Ltd, Ringwood, Victoria, Australia
Penguin Books Canada Ltd, 10 Alcorn Avenue, Toronto, Ontario, Canada M4V 3B2
Penguin Books (N.Z.) Ltd, 182–190 Wairau Road, Auckland 10, New Zealand

Penguin Books Ltd, Registered Offices: Harmondsworth, Middlesex, England

First published in the United States of America by Viking Penguin Inc., 1987
Simultaneously published in Puffin Books
Published in a Puffin Easy-to-Read edition, 1994

1 3 5 7 9 10 8 6 4 2

Text copyright © Harriet Ziefert, 1987
Illustrations copyright © Richard Brown, 1987
All rights reserved

Library of Congress Catalog Card Number: 86-82755
ISBN 0-14-036852-3

Puffin® and Easy-to-Read® are registered trademarks of Penguin Books USA Inc.
Printed in the United States of America

Reading Level 1.4

Nicky Upstairs and Down

Harriet Ziefert
Pictures by Richard Brown

PUFFIN BOOKS

Nicky lived with his mother
in a small house.

Nicky's house
had a downstairs...

and an upstairs.

When Nicky was playing,
his mother called,
"Nicky, where are you?
Are you upstairs?"

Nicky ran down the stairs.

He said, "Here I am!
I was up.
But now I'm down."

When Nicky was downstairs,
his mother called,
"Nicky, where are you?
Are you downstairs?"

Nicky ran up the stairs.

He said, "Here I am!
I was down.
But now I'm up."

Up and down.
Down and up.

Up and down the stairs —
all day long!

One day Nicky's mother called,
"Nicky, are you downstairs?"

No answer
from Nicky!

Then she called,
"Nicky, are you upstairs?"

No answer from Nicky.
No answer at all!

Nicky was hiding.
He was tired of running
up and down, down and up,
all day long!

His mother looked everywhere.
Upstairs...

and downstairs.

"Nicky," she said.
"Please come out.
Please!"

Nicky came out.
He ran halfway
up the stairs.

"Mama!" he called.
"Guess where I am?
I'm not upstairs.
I'm not downstairs."

"I'm right in the middle!"